The Tale of TWO BAD ~MICE~

by Beatrix Potter

illustrations by Unada

First printing by Worthington Press 1992.

Worthington Press
10100 SBF Drive, Pinellas Park, Florida 34666

Printed in the United States of America

2 4 6 8 10 9 7 5 3 1

ISBN 0-87406-620-4

Once upon a time there was a very
beautiful dollhouse; it was red brick with
white windows, and it had real muslin
curtains and a front door and a chimney.

It belonged to two dolls called Lucinda and Jane, at least it belonged to Lucinda, but she never ordered meals.

Jane was the cook; but she never did any cooking, because the dinner had been bought ready-made, in a box full of shavings.

There were two red lobsters and a ham, a fish, a pudding, and some pears and oranges.

They would not come off the plates, but they were extremely beautiful.

One morning Lucinda and Jane had gone
out for a drive in the doll's carriage. There
was no one in the nursery, and it was very
quiet.

Presently there was a little scuffling, scratching noise in a corner near the fireplace, where there was a hole under the skirting-board.

Tom Thumb put out his head for a moment, and then popped it in again.

Tom Thumb was a mouse.

A minute afterwards, Hunca Munca, his wife, put her head out, too; and when she saw that there was no one in the nursery, she ventured out on the oilcloth under the coal box.

The dollhouse stood at the other side of
the fireplace. Tom Thumb and Hunca
Munca went cautiously across the hearth
rug. They pushed the front door—it was
not fast.

Tom Thumb and Hunca Munca went
upstairs and peeped into the dining room.
Then they squeaked with joy!

Such a lovely dinner was laid out upon
the table! There were tin spoons, and lead
knives and forks, and two dolly chairs—all
so convenient!

Tom Thumb set to work at once to carve the ham. It was a beautiful shiny yellow, streaked with red.

The knife crumpled up and hurt him; he put his finger in his mouth.

"It is not boiled enough; it is hard. You have a try, Hunca Munca."

Hunca Munca stood up in her chair, and chopped at the ham with another lead knife.

"It's as hard as the hams at the cheese shop," said Hunca Munca.

The ham broke off the plate with a jerk, and rolled under the table.

"Let it alone," said Tom Thumb; "give me
some fish, Hunca Munca!"

Hunca Munca tried every tin spoon in
turn; the fish was glued to the dish.

Then Tom Thumb lost his temper. He put
the ham in the middle of the floor, and hit
it with the tongs and with the shovel—
bang, bang, smash, smash!

The ham flew all into pieces, for
underneath the shiny paint it was made of
nothing but plaster!

Then there was no end to the rage and disappointment of Tom Thumb and Hunca Munca. They broke up the pudding, the lobsters, the pears and the oranges.

As the fish would not come off the plate,
they put it into the red-hot crinkly paper
fire in the kitchen; but it would not burn
either.

Tom Thumb went up the kitchen chimney
and looked out at the top—there was no
soot.

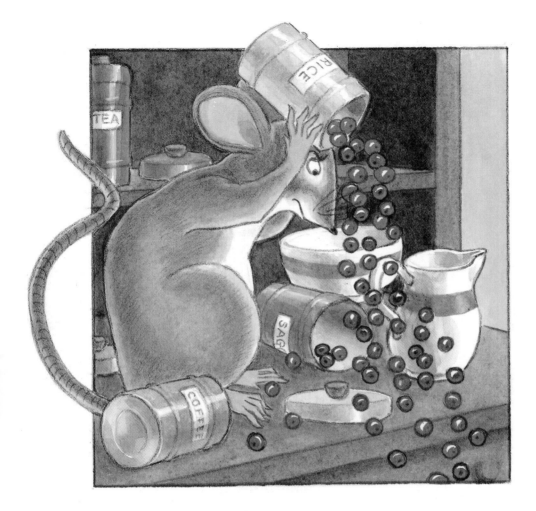

    While Tom Thumb was up the chimney,
Hunca Munca had another disappointment. She found some tiny canisters upon
the dresser, labelled—Rice—Coffee—Sago—
but when she turned them upside down,
there was nothing inside except red and
blue beads.

Then those mice set to work to do all the mischief they could—especially Tom Thumb! He took Jane's clothes out of the chest of drawers in her bedroom, and he threw them out of the top floor window.

But Hunca Munca had a frugal mind.
After pulling half the feathers out of
Lucinda's bolster, she remembered that she
herself was in want of a feather bed.

With Tom Thumb's assistance she carried
the bolster downstairs, and across the
hearth rug. It was difficult to squeeze the
bolster into the mouse hole; but they
managed it somehow.

Then Hunca Munca went back and
fetched a chair, a bookcase, a bird cage, and
several small odds and ends. The bookcase
and the bird cage refused to go into the
mouse hole.

Hunca Munca left them behind the coal box, and went to fetch a cradle.

Hunca Munca was just returning with another chair, when suddenly there was a noise of talking outside upon the landing. The mice rushed back to their hole, and the dolls came into the nursery.

What a sight met the eyes of Jane and Lucinda!

Lucinda sat upon the upset kitchen stove and stared; and Jane leaned against the kitchen dresser and smiled—but neither of them made any remark.

The bookcase and the bird cage were rescued from under the coal box—but Hunca Munca has now got the cradle, and some of Lucinda's clothes.

She also has some useful pots and pans, and several other things.

The little girl that the dollhouse belonged to, said, "I will get a doll dressed like a policeman!"

But the nurse said, "I will set a mousetrap!"

So that is the story of the two Bad Mice—
but they were not so very very naughty
after all, because Tom Thumb paid for
everything he broke.

He found a crooked sixpence under the hearth rug; and upon Christmas Eve, he and Hunca Munca stuffed it into one of the stockings of Lucinda and Jane.

And very early every morning—before anybody is awake—Hunca Munca comes with her dustpan and her broom to sweep the dollies' house!